TITLE

Reservation in Roy Cesar

1

<u>The Appointment</u>

Krissy checked out the business card she grasped. It had a name and a telephone number composed on it, in red wavy letters.

"R. Cesar. Alpha escort," she read without holding back.

Amy, her flat mate, had stuffed the card in her grasp before she left before.

"Call him, Kris, you truly need to make a move in your own hands. Have you failed to remember how you felt during your last hotness? Have you failed to remember what might have occurred? Try not to be an idiotic omega young lady, if it's not too much trouble, call the man!"

Amy's words actually waited in her mind. Goodness, she realized very well what might have occurred during her last hotness. She had been up until this point returned then, at that point, she escaped the house and wound up meandering in the city in the evening. She could undoubtedly have deteriorated. On that game changing day, right around a month prior, she had effectively been hauled by her hairs by some mischievous horny alpha, needing to have his ways with her. It was horrendous. Fortunately, Amy and her sweetheart had saved her before significantly more terrible things occurred.

She just couldn't handle herself during hotness and it just deteriorated each month. She realized she needed to remain inside her home, protected from risks, however her body didn't pay attention to her mind during one of her hotness periods and that was startling.

Presumably the absence of sex had something to do with it as well. She hadn't gotten any in right around two years. Typically, she had a fine outlook on that as she didn't want to fuck around with outsiders or have casual hookups what not, yet during heat, things changed.

Krissy realized that next Saturday would be the day: Her hotness will kick in once more.

Would it be a good idea for her she truly call this R. Cesar? Could she lay down with an outsider? A male escort...it appeared to be so off-base to do... Could she truly pay a man to impart her bed to?

This Cesar fellow was known to be a specialist when it came to omegas in heat, essentially that is the thing that Amy had said. She knew a person who knew a young lady who knew another young lady who had an incredible night with the male whore half a month back.

Krissy checked out the number and breathed in and breathed out a couple of times before she said, "guess what? To hell with it, we should do this." She then, at that point, dialed the number that was decipherable on the card. The telephone rang and a woman got.

"Goodbye, Heated administrations, this is Xelesia talking, how may I help you?"

"Uh...hello. I...I'm calling to book Mr. Cesar, for next Saturday." Krissy made a sound as if to speak. "Please." she then, at that point, added, feeling the consume on her cheeks. How can one require an escort? God, it was so ridiculously humiliating.

"Stand by one second, please." There was a brief interruption. "You will be in heat next Saturday?" Xelesia inquired. "We just take omegas in heat right now."

"Indeed, I will be."

"First day of hotness?"

"Indeed, Saturday it'll begin," Krissy replied.

"When is your pinnacle?" Xelesia inquired. "Right off the bat?"

It was practically similar to calling the specialist, aside from the way that her PCP wasn't going to bang her. Thank heavens, just the possibility of her and old Dr. Williams made her hair stand upright, and not positively.

"Definitely, the principal day. Generally in the evening," Krissy replied.

"All things considered: Saturday night will be your pinnacle?" Xelesia requested certainly.

"Indeed."

"Eight p.m., is that alright for you?"

"Y-yes."

Dear ruler. Did she truly make an appointment...?"

"Eight o'clock it is," Xelesia talked through the telephone.

The remainder of the discussion was generally Xelesia giving data. About installments, gets that should have been marked on the web, and some additional data that Krissy should wash herself before the plan occurred and to utilize toys, she ought to get them herself.

It was generally abnormal as damnation.

Furthermore that was it. Next Saturday, she would impart her bed to a male escort!

Later she had hung up the telephone, she messaged Amy to tell her that she got herself an arrangement. Amy messaged back that she was glad and that she would crash at Mason's throughout the end of the week. Artisan was Amy's beau. He was a cool person.

After five minutes, Krissy thought about what the heck she just did to herself, and she began to chuckle wildly, similar to some neurotic. "Gracious God..! What have I done?"

2

<u>Saturday</u>

Two days prior, Krissy had gotten an email from Mr. Cesar's associate, Xelesia, for certain pointers.

Like Xelesia had requested her, she had put a plastic sheet under her bedsheets for the wet wreck that could be anticipated, and on the bedside table, she had set a case of condoms. She additionally had cleaned herself completely.

It was currently practically 7.30 pm and in around thirty minutes that person, R. Cesar, would thump on her entryway to... screw her minds out. Notwithstanding, the manner in which she felt at this moment, she couldn't say whether she planned to endure another half hour.

Krissy groaned in incredible distress as she apprehensively paced before her window, wearing her white shower robe. The actual hotness began toward the beginning of today however her pinnacle began about an hour prior. She had recently washed up, however sweat was at that point dribbling from her temple once more.

For what reason did just omegas need to manage this misery? It simply wasn't reasonable, the torment that their warms caused them. Or then again the embarrassment that they felt when their first hotness out of nowhere kicked in, obviously consistently in some unacceptable spot.

What's more that was very much like how it was for Krissy when she got her first hotness. She recalled that it quite well:

It occurred in school, obviously, it needed to occur there, on that Friday evening in the absolute last hour before the chime rang. She had felt a little wiped out the entire day, however she thought it was on the grounds that she may have contracted a bug or something, however at that point, during English class, it came over her. She began perspiring and her cheeks become flushed with a more profound shade of red. At the point when she stood up, her entire pants had gotten absorbing wet one moment or thereabouts. Most cohorts snickered at her, and everything was terrible.

Around then, she didn't realize she was an omega. Evidently, she was a delayed prodigy and the main omega in the family. Her folks and three siblings were all alphas or betas.

Before that first hotness, Krissy consistently considered herself a normal beta also. Never ever did she, or any other individual, anticipated that she should be an omega.

First and foremost, in light of the fact that being an omega was not too normal. Just a modest amount of the populace was omega and for the most part they came from a line of omegas. Also besides, in light of the fact that she had no omega attributes by any means. She wasn't the supporting kind. She wasn't delicate or enthusiastic. She likewise wasn't dainty, all things being equal, she was very tall and had an enticing body shape with wide hips.

At the point when she discovered, the news hit her hard, and she had been battling about it for a long while, abhorring the reality she was unexpectedly not the same as what she suspected she'd be. It was a dim period in her life, yet presently, fortunately, she was glad once more. She was content with her life and with herself. She had likewise completely accepted her omega side.

Also this moment, she was an exceptionally horny omega. Consistently she'd fall into a thing called "heat". A period that came fourteen days before her feminine period, kind of how a beta woman got her ovulation. In any case, warms were altogether different from an ovulation. They were exceptionally extraordinary, practically carnal assuming one needed to portray the inclination with single word. In heat, bodies need to imitate, so omegas consistently get in a time of being exceptionally horny which required a couple of hours. It very well may be genuinely awful that it was truly agonizing and debilitating assuming the appetite wasn't stilled. For couples it was generally fun, sexing like monsters together, however Krissy was a solitary lady and that made it harder.

She took a gander at the clock once more. 07.50 pm.

She recently stroked off, so she ideally could accept her visitor with some mental stability before the hotness would take over again and she felt somewhat better.

Krissy cleared the perspiration off of her temple again and went to the kitchen to get a chilly brew.

It felt great when the virus drink slid through her warmed throat. Exactly when she was finished with her brew, the ringer rang and the sound made her pulse contact her throat as a shudder slithered down her spine.

This was truly going to occur. At the present time...

Goodness, God!

She strolled to the entryway and with a marginally shaking hand, she opened it.

There stood he, R. Cesar, the alpha escort.

Krissy gulped hard while she noticed the man. He looked so attractive. He was exceptionally tall and expansive. His dark hair was styled with a touch of gel and worn to the back. He wore a white shirt with the top buttons open, showing a touch of skin, and tight dark thin pants with white tennis shoes. A dark cowhide coat hung nonchalantly over his shoulders. He appeared to be great with agreeable eyes as he grinned.

Krissy anticipated a man, wearing a slick suit or something however she enjoyed this more.

"Can I possibly come in?" he asked while they remained there for two or three abnormal seconds, making Krissy wake up from her gaze.

"Gracious! Indeed... Indeed, certain, come in!" she said, making a move to the side to give the alpha access. God, he had such a lovely aroma, and Krissy took in profoundly a couple of times.

The man brought his hand towards her. "I'm Roy Cesar, ideal to meet you."

Roy? Roy Cesar. The name sounded recognizable yet Krissy couldn't recall where she heard it previously and the present moment she wasn't in the situation to think plainly as she was unable to gather by any means.

"Krissy," she said while shaking Roy's solid hand, reviling herself that she offered such a powerless sweat-soaked hand herself. She then, at that point, scoured her sweat-soaked hands on her shower robe. "I...I never did this," she said anxiously. "I don't have a clue how it functions. That is to say, s-would it be advisable for us we go to the room?" She gulped. "Or then again.. would you like something to drink first?"

"We should go to the lounge room first, we can talk a bit," Roy answered.

A couple of moments later, they were having a lager and a little talk.

"You're not what I was anticipating that you should be," Krissy said.

"No? What were you anticipating then, at that point?" Roy asked, grinning.

"Uhh... somebody looking more... I don't have a clue. Possibly more like a player or something like that? You resemble a typical person. That is to say, you're attractive, I don't intend to say you're uglier than a player, cause you're not. You're very hot, and I'm happy you appear as though you do, uhh, hot, I mean. In any case, uhh...I'm sorry..." Krissy continued meandering aimlessly, advising herself to quiet down as her mouth continued onward.

She felt a blush consume her cheeks. It very well may be disgrace or it very well may be heat kicking in once more.

Roy laughed. "Unwind, please. You don't need to be so apprehensive and you don't need to be embarrassed all things considered. I totally comprehend the reason why you booked me."

"You do?"

"Definitely... It's difficult for omegas to be in heat," the alpha said, so understanding.

"It is," Krissy concurred. "Truth be told, I believe I'm additionally this anxious on the grounds that I haven't had intercourse in right around two years."

"Amazing... that is quite a while. I feel exceptionally regarded that you picked me to take care of you."

Krissy giggled a piece ungracefully before she felt it: a rush of hotness flooding through her body again and a spasm hitting her in her stomach. Unexpectedly, the infiltrating fragrance of the alpha reclining across from her hit her like a huge load of block and she felt the blood inside her body being siphoned to her face and a specific region between her legs, causing her clothing to saturate once more.

"Well," she groaned, feeling the spasms, and wanting to. It was the ideal opportunity for her hotness to be taken care of.

Roy stood up, and gradually he strolled to Krissy, offering her his hand. It was the ideal opportunity for the alpha escort to get right into it.

3
<u>Freeding The Heat</u>

Krissy smelled that Roy got more excited and that summoned further sentiments inside her once more, similar to a chain response: They both got hornier from one another's aromas. Thus, she readily acknowledged Roy's introduced hand and stood up.

"Walk us to the room," the alpha arranged in a profound voice, to which Krissy gestured, and her nerves were supplanted by unadulterated desire and expectation when she pondered how this man could deal with her.

Once inside the room, Roy looked for the light switch, clicked it on, and darkened the unforgiving light a little.

"Is this alright?" he inquired.

Krissy gestured. She can't muster enough willpower to care assuming that it was light or dull. She just felt hot, consuming hot, similar to she was ablaze and she really wanted to take a gander at Roy with weighty lidded eyes. An asking look, without a doubt.

He got her shoulders and pushed her against the divider, squeezing his nose against her neck fragrance organ, and breathed in profound. Krissy could hear him murmur with fulfillment as his hot breath fanned against her neck and a tongue ran up from her neck to her ear, snacking on the little flap.

"I will make you start things out, alright? To take a large portion of the strain off for the present," the alpha inhaled against the shell of her ear.

"Gee," Krissy groaned, horny as heck, before she felt a knee squeezing her legs more extensive, while Roy's hand pulled at the line of her wraparound. He pushed the garment from her body till it tumbled to the ground and a tad.

"So hot," he said and put his hand on top of her doused underwear while he kissed her lips and delicately pushed his tongue between them, twisting it around her's.

They began kissing and salivation and breaths were shared and blended as Krissy gasped and groaned into the alpha's mouth, becoming insane with that stroking hand. She was feeling way too hotly and woozy to contemplate the reality a sex-specialist was contacting her most private spot.

Her body simply needed delivery so seriously.

The hand that had been touching, slid inside the trim texture and crawled against the warm damped wetness between her legs.

"Hahh...!" she heaved into Roy's mouth, her hands grasping at his shirt.

The alpha licked her neck, collarbones, and bosoms while his fingers gathered a portion of her smooth, till his hand was drenching wet.

"You're overall quite wet," he inhaled against her warmed skin while his fingers thought that she is throbbing clit and did something amazing.

Krissy folded her arms over his neck and pulled Roy closer. She needed to feel him close, just só close, to smell his wonderful aroma loaded up with alpha hornyness.

She groaned while his fingers accelerated their speed, drawing circles over the round little solidifying dab, making her breathing speed up.

"I'm want to taste you, can I?" Roy inquired.

Krissy gulped. "Y-yes," she gestured as Roy looked at her without flinching.

Fuck, yes.

The alpha raised her up, her absorbing pussy dirtying his fresh white shirt, however he didn't appear to be troubled. He strolled to the bed and tenderly positioned her down.

He removed his shirt and furthermore took Krissy's breath during the time spent doing that. He was so frikking stunning. Built, yet not to an extreme, simply the manner in which she preferred it.

He then, at that point, kissed her again and before long nestled his direction down, his nose brushing all around her steaming hot body as his teeth touched over her areolas and his tongue licking over her tummy.

"Oh...!" Krissy let out when Roy culled off her underwear and tossed them in some side of the room.

He kissed her tummy and her legs, applauding her between each kiss: "You're...a...very...beautiful...woman...Krissy..." he said until his mouth shut around her most delicate spot and he delicately began sucking at her clit while his fingers slid inside till they were covered knuckle-somewhere inside her hotness.

"Ahh...!" Krissy let out an uproarious groan and balled her clench hands as she felt the way his lips, tongue, and mouth chipped away at her body like the master that R. Cesar was known for.

She was glad that Amy knew a young lady who knew a person who knew a young lady who knew another young lady and had suggested him.

Blessed Fuck, this was at that point the best excitement she'd at any point gotten and barely anything had even occurred at this point!

Disgraceful groans and corrupt slurping commotions skiped off the room dividers as her shaking hands got Roy by his hair.

"I...I...ahh," she gasped, feeling her stomach as of now fix and her toes twisting later not so much as 1 moment.

She pushed her hips needily against his tongue, which musically hovered over her pulsating clit before she peaked. Roy licked her through the climax and halted when her muscles were finished grasping around his fingers before he gradually slid up again and laid close to her, pulling her in his arms, and allowing her head to lay on his chest.

Krissy felt tacky and sweat-soaked thus, so hot, yet she adored that he took her in his arms like this. Obviously, it was every one of the an exterior, Roy was paid to do this, yet, it felt pleasant regardless.

"How can you feel?" the man inquired.

Krissy snickered a piece ungracefully before she replied. "I feel extraordinary."

"Great. I'm hanging around for you. In the event that you need or need something or don't need me to accomplish something, tell me. Alright?" Roy inquired.

"I will."

They laid like that for some time. Krissy saw that Roy calmly delayed until her need took over again and he really at that time drifted over her and began kissing and touching her once more.

"I need to feel you inside," she said and felt quickly embarrassed she just exclaimed those words. She just couldn't resist. She needed to feel his fat bunch inside her.

"It'll be my pleasure," Roy murmured. "It's what I'm here for..."

4
<u>First Heat</u>

WHEN SHE FOUND OUT HER PANTS WERE SOAKING WET, THE POOR OMEGA HASTED OUT OF THE CLASSROOM. CONFUSED, SHE RAN THROUGH THE SCHOOL BUILDING, LEAVING A TRACE OF SWEET OMEGA-PERFUME IN THE HALLWAYS.

THE OTHER STUDENTS WERE ALL CONFUSED WITH THE PENETRATING, BUT DELICIOUS SCENT WHEN IT CAME CRAWLING UP THEIR NOSES BECAUSE THEY'D NEVER SMELLED THE PHEROMONES OF AN OMEGA IN HEAT BEFORE, FOR ALL OMEGAS USED TO ATTEND A SPECIAL ALL OMEGA SCHOOL.

KRISSY QUICKLY ESCAPED THE SCHOOL BUILDING BUT HAD TO STOP IN FRONT OF IT, TO CATCH BACK HER BREATH.

"WHAT THE FUCK IS HAPPENING?" SHE PANTED. "AM...AM I IN F-FUCKING HEAT?!" SHE ASKED HERSELF, CONFUSED AND SOFTLY BEGAN TO CRY.

AN ALPHA GUY WHO'D SEEN AND HEARD IT ALL APPROACHED HER. HE WAS CHUBBY, HAD BLACK HAIR, AND WORE THICK BLACK GLASSES. HIS EYES BEHIND THE GLASS LOOKED AT HER WITH SYMPATHY.

KRISSY WAS INTIMIDATED BY HIM IN THE VULNERABLE STATE SHE WAS IN, BUT SHE WAS ALSO ATTRACTED TO THE SOOTHING SCENT THAT CAME FROM THE GUY.

"HERE," HE SAID AS HE HANDED KRISSY HIS JACKET. "YOU CAN TIE THAT AROUND YOUR WAIST."

"THANKS," KRISSY SAID, THANKFUL SHE HAD SOMETHING TO COVER THE LARGE WET STAIN.

"PLEASE, LET ME TAKE YOU HOME, MY CAR IS RIGHT THERE," THE ALPHA SAID, POINTING AT HIS VEHICLE.

WHAT SHOULD SHE DO NOW? COULD SHE JUST GO WITH HIM? WHAT IF THIS GUY WAS BAD NEWS? MAYBE SHE SHOULD CALL HER MOM INSTEAD?

JUST AS SHE THOUGHT HER OPTIONS THROUGH, ANOTHER CRAMP HIT HER AND SHE STARTED SWEATING.

"PLEASE, YES, TAKE ME HOME." SHE DIDN'T FEEL GOOD AT ALL, SO SHE AGREED TO THE ALPHA'S SUGGESTION OF COMING WITH HIM.

HE SEEMED LIKE HE COULD BE TRUSTED, SO KRISSY HOPED SHE DIDN'T MAKE A MISTAKE BY STEPPING INTO THE SILVER CAR.

"YOU WANT SOME WATER?" THE GUY ASKED WHILE DRIVING.

"YES, YOU HAVE ANY FOR ME?'

"IN MY BAG. YOU CAN OPEN IT YOURSELF," HE SAID
WHILE BREATHING HEAVILY. "I'M SORRY, I NEED TO
BREATHE THROUGH MY MOUTH BECAUSE THE SCENT
THAT'S COMING FROM YOUR SCENT GLANDS IS
GETTING STRONGER AND STRONGER."

"OH...I-I'M SORRY," KRISSY SAID, AS SHE LOOKED
THROUGH THE BAG. SHE FOUND THE BOTTLE OF
WATER AND YANKED THE LID OFF BEFORE SHE
DRANK IT UP IN ONE GO. GOSH, THAT FELT GOOD.

"YOU DON'T HAVE TO BE SORRY, BUT YOU DO HAVE
TO GIVE ME DIRECTIONS TO YOUR HOUSE," THE
ALPHA SAID.

"HERE TO THE LEFT," KRISSY REPLIED BEFORE A
SUDDEN MOAN ESCAPED HER MOUTH. "AHHH...SHIT!
HMM..."

SHE CLUTCHED AT THE DASHBOARD. WHAT THE
FUCK WAS HAPPENING? IT REALLY SEEMED LIKE SHE
WAS IN HEAT. HOW WAS ALL THIS POSSIBLE?

"ARE... ARE YOU OK?!"

"NO, I'M FUCKING NOT OK!" KRISSY BARKED,
INSTANTLY REGRETTING IT. "I...I'M SORRY. I DIDN'T
MEAN TO YELL AT YOU."

SHE KNEW THE GUY ONLY WANTED TO HELP HER.
SHE DIDN'T MEAN TO SCREAM AT HIM.

"IT'S FINE, I UNDERSTAND," HE REPLIED.

KRISSY WIPED SOME SWEAT FROM HER FOREHEAD."TO THE RIGHT, THEN NEXT STREET TO THE LEFT."

THE SCENT OF THE DRIVER WAS SO DIVINE THAT KRISSY NEEDED TO RESTRAIN HERSELF FROM DIVING INTO THAT APPEALING NECK AND SNIFF HIM ALL OVER. SHE MOANED AND LOOKED MORTIFIED AT HER OWN CROTCH WHEN SHE FELT A WAVE OF SLICK DRIPPING OUT.

"THERE, THAT WHITE HOUSE!" SHE CRIED OUT, NEEDING TO GET OUT OF THIS CAR NOW. LIKE, RIGHT NOW!

AFTER THE CAR STOPPED WITH SQUEALING TIRES, SHE QUICKLY GOT OUT AND SCREAMED: "THANKS!"

SHE WOULD RETURN THE JACKET TOMORROW AND THANK THE BOY PROPERLY THEN, BUT RIGHT, NOW SHE WAS IN A HURRY TO GET HOME.

~

HOWEVER, WHEN KRISSY RETURNED TO SCHOOL A WEEK LATER, WITHIN HER HANDS A FRESHLY WASHED JACKET, THE ALPHA WASN'T THERE.

HE NEVER SHOWED UP AT SCHOOL AGAIN.

KRISSY LATER FOUND OUT THAT HER SAVIOR HAD MOVED TO ANOTHER CITY AND WAS TRANSFERRED TO ANOTHER SCHOOL.

SHE NEVER GOT TO THANK HIM...

======================================

Roy broke our kiss and took off his pants, socks, and boxer
briefs. When I saw his erected penis pointing in my
direction, I was shocked, to say the least. It was fucking huge
with thick veins running up the shaft, bulging underneath
his skin. It's been two years since I saw a cock in this state,
and it turned me on very, VERY much.
"Oh, God!"

Wait...did I just say that out loud?
Roy smiled at my reaction and that smirk only made me feel
hotter than I already felt.

His tongue started to explore my breasts, sliding over my
nipples, sucking them till they were stiff in his mouth. When
he gently nibbled at one, I let my hands roam over his body.
I loved his muscles. They felt hard, yet his skin was soft.
God, he smelled so good.

He kissed his way up and pried my lips open with his tongue
which he twirled against mine, making me a moaning mush
underneath him again.

His cock pressed between my legs and it really was *sohorny.*

"Ahh," I moaned at a sudden cramp.

I wanted him so badly and I couldn't help myself but grab
him. I just needed to. A hissing sound came from him when I
squeezed the hard veiny shaft inside my hand. My palm wet
from his pre-cum.

He really was big. I mean… really massive!

Could this even fit inside me? Probably yes, otherwise he couldn't do his job, but…my thumb and index finger weren't even touching when I held the huge flesh in my hand.

Oh, dear… I didn't know if I wanted to get wrecked by him or run out of this room, panicking as I watched him rolling a condom on it.

I didn't need to think about it for long, though, because a wave of heat hit me again and I became in that feverish state once more, sweat gushing from my temples.

Roy grabbed my legs and spread them wide. He then rubbed his hand over his scent gland and pushed it gently against my nose, smearing his fragrance over my face.

I couldn't describe what I felt at that moment. My toes curled, only from that scent and I felt a stream of slick oozing out of me. Thank goodness for that plastic sheet under the bedsheets.
I was a wet mess.

"Ahhh….G-God…" I almost choked.

"Relax, Krissy," he ordered as he positioned himself between my legs. "I'll make you feel good, trust me."

His hands coated his cock with my fluids before I felt the throbbing head between my inner lips.

"Ahh…Fuck me, please!" I begged.

5

<u>New Client</u>

When a regular client of mine had canceled her Saturday appointment, I was actually pleased because I really wanted to catch up with my friend Kevin, who would celebrate his birthday that day. I had been bummed out I couldn't go but the cancelation made it possible again.

However, he just called to let me know that the party was canceled because his sweet woman had gone into labor! She was thirty-seven weeks pregnant, so I guess they got themselves an impatient baby. I smiled thinking about the fact that he would be the first in our group of friends to become a father. I was so happy for him and his girlfriend and I hoped the birth of his first child would go well and smoothly.

"Boss, I have a call for next Saturday. Shall I book it?"

Making me a free man again, I told Xelesia that she could book the appointment and thirty minutes later, she handed me the client's file.

The client was a lady who shall have her peak next Saturday evening. She was twenty-seven years old, the same age as I was. Nothing unusual until I saw something that made my heart skip a beat or two:

Her name. *Krissy Waters.*

My mouth slammed open at that very moment and the coffee in my hand landed on my lap. I was too flabbergasted to even curse myself for dropping it. Luckily, it wasn't scalding hot anymore as my whole pants were soaking wet.

"What?" I questioned myself after two minutes of disbelief. "How?"

What were the odds? I mean...it was her! And she only got this appointment because my other client had canceled and Kevin's baby had decided to come three weeks earlier than she was supposed to come.

And cancellations were rare to happen, I hardly had gotten any in these past few years. Yet, right when I did got one, *she* came on my path again. I just couldn't comprehend how this was possible! It had to be faith, there simply was no other explanation for it!

So many times I'd dreamed about seeing her again, even if it was only a glimpse, even if I could only see her crossing the street somewhere. That would already have been enough.

My thoughts went back to the last time I ever saw her. The scene that had played in my head at least a million times:

"THANKS!" SHE SHOUTED TO ME AS SHE RAN TO HER DOOR, AND TRIED TO OPEN IT WITH TREMBLING HANDS THIRTY SECONDS LATER.

I FELT SO MANY THINGS. I PITIED HER, I WAS WORRIED FOR HER, SHOCKED THAT SHE WAS AN OMEGA, HORNY BY HER SCENT. I WAS HAPPY TO SPEND TIME WITH HER IN MY CAR, WHERE HER SCENT STILL LINGERED. I BREATHED IN DEEP. GOD, SHE SMELLED SO GOOD!

SHE STEPPED THROUGH THE DOOR AND SLAMMED IT SHUT. LUCKILY SHE WAS HOME. THIS MUST BE SO STRANGE AND DIFFICULT FOR HER.

I STARTED MY ENGINE AND TOOK OFF, FEELING HAPPY I COULD BE THE ONE TO HELP HER THIS TIME. THE NEXT TIME I WILL SEE HER AT SCHOOL, THIS DEFINITELY GAVE ME A REASON TO TALK TO HER AND THAT GAVE ME A SMILE ON MY FACE.

LITTLE DID I KNOW I WOULD NEVER SEE HER AT SCHOOL AGAIN...

"Seven years..." I mumbled to myself while holding the file in my trembling hands.

I hadn't seen her in seven years! Her face, however, I could still vividly see in front of me. I could picture every detail of it.

She didn't really know me, but I knew her very well. I knew all about her. Every day, I watched her whenever I had the chance. She was the highlight of a school day for me. She was the reason I got out of bed in the morning and the last thing on my mind before I went to sleep. She was my first crush, and the heaviest crush I'd ever had. My love was never answered, but how could it be answered, I'd never told her my feelings.

We were in different classes but while having lunch or in the hallways, I could catch a glimpse of her, and it made my whole day great again. Even if the glimpse only lasted a second.

I looked a little different back in those days. I was chubby, wore thick glasses and my skin wasn't all to well either. My confidence was absolutely zero.

Luckily, I had a nice group of friends, but I was always the one that nobody noticed. Not like Kevin with his muscled body or Peter with his cool attitude. Blake had the humor and Tim knew his fashion, and then there was me.

One day, I was in a bad, bad mood, feeling so useless and lonely. That was also the day that I first noticed her. She came up to me and asked why I was sulking so badly. We talked a little, and it was nice. When she left, my mood was a lot better. I'd been surprised, she returned after ten minutes, and gave me my favorite drink.

"SORRY, THIS WAS ALL THEY HAD, I HOPE YOU LIKE IT," she had said.

That act of kindness made me fall for her.

I wondered how she looked now, what her life was like... She probably didn't have a partner, otherwise, she wouldn't come to see me. That thought made me happy.

I swallowed hard when it finally hit me what I was booked for. I GOT TO... Oh, God, the things I could do to her, the things I would do to her...

My heart actually hurt, as it beat wildly inside my chest, and I clutched onto my shirt at the height of the fast beating organ.

"Jesus, calm down, Roy."

Then, suddenly, fear took hold of me. What if she knew it was me and was disappointed at what I did in life? I was an escort after all. It wasn't like I was disappointed in myself at all, I did this because I liked it, because I actually helped people. But I didn't want HER to feel disappointed in me.

==================================

"Ahh," she moaned, and every time she did, it reminded me of what I was actually doing:

Having sex with my first ever crush.

To be fair, I think I had fallen for her all over again from the moment she'd opened the door, earlier this evening.

And fuck, how she felt so good. She was soft, and beautiful and so, SO sexy and her scent almost was the death of me, just like her soaking pussy was that currently slithered against my cock.

Jesus Christ! A hiss spilled from my lips as her tongue licked over my ear while one of her hands grabbed my cock, and explored it a little. I let her squeeze and caress it a bit before I kneeled, grabbed a condom from the bedside table, and rolled it on.

Feeling excited like a kid in a candy store, I couldn't wait to bury myself inside her warmth.
I knew that I probably would feel like shit after this evening, because I might never see her again, but right now, she was here, and so was I.

I felt her tremble and knew she was having it hard again. It was up to me to make her feel better and that was exactly what I was planning to do, making her feel better by fucking her like there was no tomorrow. She'll never forget the man called Roy Cesar ever again, that was one thing I promised myself as I spread her legs and admired the view for a moment.

HOLY SHIT. It made me almost choke on my own saliva.

One thing I knew omegas loved, was the scent trick. I bet Krissy was no different, so, I rubbed my hand over my scent gland and onto her face and watched her eyes roll back while her pussy drizzled for me. It was the horniest thing I'd ever seen.

"Ahhh....G-god..." she said, breathlessly.

"Relax, Krissy," I replied as I took my place between her legs. "I'll make you feel good, trust me."

I then coated my dick with her slick and pressed my dick against her heat, inhaling her perfume of desires.

"Ahh...Fuck me, please!" she begged.

6

<u>Knotting</u>

"Ahhh, Roy!" she gasped when I entered her. I swear to God, I almost came right then and there. And how lame would that have been, being a professional sex-worker? Thank goodness, I just controlled myself.

She grabbed my body tight till I felt the burn of her scratching fingernails edging into the skin of my back while she buried her nose against my neck, deeply inhaling my fragrance. She clenched around me. It drove me insane, she drove me insane. It felt like I entered paradise itself.

I've had a lot of sex in my life but I can honestly say that I've never felt this way when I was on the job. In fact, I've never felt this way*ever* while when having sex with someone! It felt just so right.

She let her head relax on the pillow while pulling my face towards her before she planted her lips on my mouth, her tongue pushing between my lips.

I let her adjust a little and took it slow because two years of no sex was a long time and after a short moment, I felt her slowly relaxing her muscles. Hands flattened down on my back, no more pointy nails.

I withdrew my cock till it was almost out of her and pushed back in. *Jesus Christ*, I had to fight against my own feelings. If I wouldn't control myself, I'd form my knot too soon, or worse: mark her here and now.

~~~KRISSY~~~

Needy, that was the word to describe how I felt right now. I needed him inside me so badly.

Hearing him growl into my ear was hot. His scent was hot. The sound of his cock thrusting into me was hot. He was hot. I felt hot.

The idea that I had booked an escort to fuck me still felt so surreal, but the thrusts of his hips that fucked me hard into the bedsheets at the moment reminded me that this was, in fact, very real.

Roy licked his way back to my neck and nibbled and sucked at the skin below my ear. It has always been a weak spot for me. I moaned loudly when he sped up his pace and clamped my body against his. My knees clutched against his hips and my hands pulled his face closer, so I could kiss him again. I loved the way he kissed me, so full of passion. I don't think I've ever felt more desired than right now.

I made sounds I'd never heard before. High pitched moans and low guttural grunts.

"Ahh...harder," I breathed against his lips, begging him for more while our breaths mingled. As much as I loved this pace, I wanted him faster, deeper, and rougher.

He purred into my ear when all of a sudden, the full feeling left me, and it instantly made me want to scream my lungs out with frustration. Two strong hands then pulled me up to sit, turned me around, and pushed me on the bed again, before they grabbed my ass, lifted it high in the air and with a deep growl, he invaded me again.

"Ahh!" I cried out, sitting on all fours with him kneeling behind me, taking me hard.

His balls swung and slammed against my lips with every thrust he made. Skin slapping on skin. He fucked me exactly how I liked to be fucked, at the right pace while one of his hands found my clit again and his fingers started to rub in circles while he never once slowed down.

I grabbed the sheets, my knuckles turning pale, and my fingers growing numb before I cried out again, my orgasm on the verge.

I turned my head around and looked at him, his image mirroring mine: red blushing skin and shimmering with sweat.

Then I felt it.

His cock expanded inside me, becoming even fatter than it already was until his knot was fully formed and was now locking us together. I've never been knotted before and it felt so intense when I surrendered to this blissful feeling.

Moans and heavy breaths bounced off my bedroom walls and I felt electricity run down my spine when a wave of goosebumps took over my body and my eyes rolled up into my skull when my orgasm was there. I saw stars and almost choked on my own saliva while I came, experiencing the most intense climax I've ever had.

He grunted hard after a deep thrust and I knew he was there as well. I felt his member throb inside of me with each shot his cock squirted into the rubber.

It felt like the longest orgasm I've ever had and afterwards, I collapsed on the bed, completely drained and laying into my own wetness. Roy fell on top of me while still locked inside.

When my high ebbed away, Roy rolled us over, until we laid on our sides, him spooning me from behind. We needed to wait until his knot was gone before we could separate. It was so strange how my body was instantly calmed down. It got what it had craved for and I felt at peace. Finally.

Roy caressed my belly and nuzzled the back of my head, his nose rubbing in my hair when I felt myself doze off, but only half. It was like I was in some sort of ultra-relaxing state while I felt his soft hands touching me so gently, and so lovingly, over and over again.

Half asleep, I laughed.

"What is it?" Roy asked.

"I understand why people like you so much," I replied, my eyes still shut. It was pure bliss for me right now.

"You liked it?" Roy asked.

"The fucking? Oh yes," I answered. "But not just that. I also like this."

"You do?"

"Yeah...us, laying together like this. You make me feel like it's not just a paid fuck. I know it is, and I know it sounds dumb but...I feel...important right now. Like you're taking care of me as a real boyfriend would do. I know it's stupid to think like that because this is just an illusion, something I'm paying for." I should stop myself right now. I didn't even know why I was telling him all of this. "I'm sorry if I'm saying weird stuff. I'm just so tired..."

"Shhh, sleep then." I heard the alpha whisper in my ear as he held me tight and so gentle.

7

<u>**The Morning after**</u>

Krissy opened her eyes. Rays of sunlight came peeking through the curtains, and felt warm against her face. She felt better, the extreme feelings that came with her heat were gone.

Two strong arms hugged around her. Roy was still there.

She debated what to do now. Should she wake up the alpha? The man probably wanted to go home as soon as possible as the job was done.

However, Krissy was being a little bit selfish, so she closed her eyes again, and cuddled up against the alpha, pretending to sleep. It felt so good when Roy held her even tighter in his arms.

When was the last time she'd laid like this with someone? Hugging like this. Oh yeah: never.

She never had a relationship before. She had flings and some dates and a couple of one night stands, even a fuck buddy once. But for some reason they'd never spent the whole night. There were never any feelings involved. And though

Roy didn't have any feelings for her either, it was nice to pretend a little.

She wiggled her behind against the alpha, trying to make a little nest-like feeling against him, when Roy sighed and mumbled with a sleepy voice:

"If you keep going on with what you are doing, I'm afraid I must show you my services once more..."

Krissy swallowed hard when she heard the voice and knew Roy wasn't sleeping anymore. A hard bulge grew against her bum and she smelled a familiar scent.

"Oh," Krissy said, breathing in Roy's horny fragrance.

"Yeah..." Roy relied.

*~~~ **KRISSY** ~~~*

I felt the warm water slide over my body when taking a shower. It was Sunday five o'clock in the afternoon already, and Roy was still here!

We just finished another "session". I couldn't believe he took me again. I only paid the man till three at night, it was now fourteen hours later, but he stayed anyway.

I felt my face burn when I thought about this morning. It was very different from last night. At night, I was in heat and when I'm in heat, I could never think clearly. No limits, no shame. I just wanted to climax over and over again, selfishly, not caring about the other. Just me and my need.

But this morning... When I felt him harden against me, I grew horny as fuck, wanting to pleasure him as well. Before he could touch me, my face was under the sheets already, taking him in my mouth.

The man must think so little of me now. Gosh, I was so shameless! How is it even possible that I was so needy after such a wild night?

I snapped out of my thoughts as I heard a knock on the door. After turning off the water, I answered, "Yes?"

"Krissy, I need to leave in about ten minutes," Roy spoke on the other side of the door.

"Ok, I'll be right out."

I wanted to at least say goodbye to him so I quickly dried myself and got dressed. My teeth, I'd already brushed under the shower. When I was done, I found Roy in the kitchen.

"I made you some late lunch. Eat. And drink, please. You definitely need to drink after last night."

He made me a meal? What kind of service is this? I felt a little guilty knowing his fees were not that high. Why did he go through all this trouble? I truly felt like a Queen.

"Wow, Roy... You didn't have to do this," I said.

"No, I didn't, but I wanted to," he replied while getting his stuff to head home.

"Oh...ok...Well, thank you!" I said and he smiled while we walked to the door.

"So, uhhh... thank you for your...services."

Gosh this was awkward...

Roy smiled again. This man was just so handsome and sweet and gentle.Why did he have to be an escort?! Why couldn't I just meet him in a bar or at the train station or somewhere else? Why?

"You really don't recognize me, do you?" he asked.

"Huh?" Wait? What?

Suddenly, my first feeling of when I met him came back to me. His face had seemed familiar when I opened up the door, I remembered it very clearly now. The rest of our time together, I hadn't thought about it anymore. I'd also always been really bad with remembering faces.

"Roy, do we know each other?"

"We do."

"From where?" I asked, full of curiosity.

"From a while back. I will have you figure it out yourself."

"What? No! I will never be able too!" I whined. He couldn't do this to me. If I wanted to know something, I couldn't let it go.

"Yes you will, I know you will."

He looked at the side-table beside the door where a roll of cash laid waiting for him. Xelesia had mailed me that I needed to handle the payment like that: Leave cash at the front door, so Roy didn't have to ask for it. That way, it would be less awkward for us both

He reached for it, or at least, that's what I thought he did, but instead, he took the stack of post-its and a pen that also laid there.

"Here," he said after writing something down and peeling the upper post-it off and sticking it to my chest.

I plucked it off. "Your phone number?"

"Yes, my private one. Message me if you have figured it out," he said, opened the door and took off.

"Wait, Roy!" I raised my voice.

"I don't want it, keep it!" he yelled back, without turning his head.

I looked at the roll of money in my hand. What the...?

~

After losing sleep for almost three days, guessing where I knew Roy from, I experienced an epiphany. The schoolbooks! He had said that we knew each other from a while back, so it could be from school.

After spitting through a few books without success, I opened up the last one.

I laughed at my own photo. And there was Amy. Ahh, we looked so young and cute

It was the year in which my life had changed so dramatically. The year where I turned out to be an omega. I turned the page and let my eyes fall on a guy with glasses.

"No fucking way!!!" I screamed. "Roy is chubby savior guy?!"

I looked at the face of a boy that indeed looked like Roy, but then also...not at all. This boy had very chubby cheeks, a big roll under his chin and the most ugly black plastic glasses on his nose. Just an overall expression that screamed "NERD".

After staring at the photo for a few minutes and recalling the day back that I had seen him for the last time, I grabbed my phone.

I figured it out.

Wow... I never expected it to be you. I can't believe I didn't recognize you! I never got to thank you properly and I would like to do that. Maybe you don't know it, but you were a lifesaver back then and I never forgot you. Though...it appeared I did forget you, because you were

standing right in front of my face and I didn't even see it! I feel so lame right now...I really would like to talk to you again, if you would like it too, please let me thank you.

I looked at my text and deleted it all.

"That sounds so dumb."

I wrote again.

Roy, I can't believe you were the chubby nerdy guy!

"Ugh no!"

Why should I call the guy fat in a text? That's just rude.

Roy, I finally know who you are. It took me three days, but I figured it out. Can we please talk in person?

That's better. I smiled and hit send.

8

<u>Unco-operative</u>

Roy had a huge smile pasted to his face while sitting in his car in front of Krissy's apartment. He just had the best night and day of his life.

He laughed out loud knowing he acted like a moron but he couldn't help it. He was happy after spending time with her even though he knew he probably would never receive someone's love as long as he kept doing what he did. Like Krissy would ever like him, an escort! He loved his job, but for the right person he would give it up in a heartbeat if he knew there was even the tiniest chance of having a serious relationship, and right now, tiny little glimpses of hope filled up his heart. Maybe Krissy could be that right person. He could only wait and hope that Krissy could guess who he was and would contact him.

The smile on his face vanished. Why was he so stupid? He should just have told Krissy right away who he was. Why didn't he?

"Ach, such an idiot!" he cried out and let his head drop on the steering wheel.

~

"Roy, hun, what's wrong? Are you maybe having some stress?" a lady asked after having done everything in her power to arouse her escort for the day. His cock simply wouldn't grow for her.

"Fuck! Milly, it's not working." Roy was so mortified. About the worst thing that could happen to a male escort just happened to him. Or better said; something didn't happen that should've happened...

He couldn't get a stiffy, he couldn't get it up! No boner, no hard-on, no erection, no rod of steal, nothing! Just a soft lump of flesh, it stayed.

Milly, his client, came up from underneath the sheets again.

"I'm so s-sorry, Milly...I...ugh," Roy shamefully stuttered.

Milly was one of his regular clients, one that he saw for a very long time already. One that had the privilege of booking him without heat and thank God, she wasn't in heat, because then he would have a real guilt problem.

"It's ok, hun," she said kindly.

"Please, I know this is lame to say but it's true: It's not you, it's me and I'm *so* sorry. Obviously, you don't have to pay me tonight. Of course, you don't!"

Roy sighed and ran his fingers through his thick black hair. He pulled up the sheets and looked at his useless cock which laid lifeless on his leg, still shimmering with her spit.

"You want me to try it with my mouth again?" she asked while looking at him with eyes full of sympathy.

"I don't think it will work, Mil...but...thanks."

She patted his shoulder. "Don't feel so bad. I know this thing never happened to you before. If it's not stress, there must be another reason. Are you perhaps having feelings for someone?"

"You think that could have anything to do with it?" Roy asked her with wide eyes.

She smiled. Milly was older than him, about 45 years old and Roy always thought she was a very wise woman. He respected her a lot.

"Does this mean I'm right and you indeed have feelings for somebody?"

Roy nodded. His feelings were the same as they were all those years ago. Krissy was in his mind all day and night, since those 3 days ago. He hadn't heard from the woman since, and it felt awful.

Roy had dreaded coming to this appointment too. He took days off for the past 2 days, and this was his first time on the job after the night with Krissy. Roy knew nothing could ever beat that experience.

"I'm very happy for you."

"Well, you don't have to be happy for now, because I haven't told that person how I felt. At least not yet."

"Being in love is still beautiful. I think you should tell that person. And I think you need to take a break from this until you do. If you love someone, then go for it, Roy. As for now, I think we should get dressed.”

The alpha didn't like to leave her hanging like this.

“Are you sure? I mean…I could go down on you if you want. There is nothing wrong with my tongue or fingers and I know how much you like it when I do that…”

She laughed hard. “Thanks, but no thanks. The spark is gone, Roy. You just figure your stuff out. As much as I love sleeping with you, I hope you'll find true love first. Love always comes first.”

She stood up and put her clothes back on.

“Can you zip me up?” she asked standing before him in her black dress.

“Yeah, sure.”

“Ok, I'm out,” Milly said while she picked up her purse and walked to the door. “The room has been paid for till 6. Sleep some, relax some. All the best to you, hun, and if your love doesn't work out, call me when you are feeling good to go again.” With a wink, Milly left the room and Roy remained laying on the bed, feeling sorry for himself. And for the poor woman.

He pulled up the sheets again and looked down. “Are you gonna refuse everyone else now? Hm?” he asked his dick.

He closed his eyes and thought about Krissy's face. Those heavy-lidded eyes when she came hard because of him. Because of his cock inside of her. He started rubbing his own balls a little, and, poof! Yes, there it was, he was erected after a second. His cock was hard as a brick with only the girl's face in his mind, while Milly couldn't even get it up by sucking on it. And that was something that never had happened before, Milly was normally one of his favorite clients. She was good at blow jobs too.

But not as good as...

Milly was right. It was because of his feelings for Krissy. He couldn't get it up for other people anymore, only for Krissy. What should he do now? How must he keep up with this job when he can't perform.

What if this happens with someone in heat? Or some insecure girl who finally had the guts to call him to lose their virginity? And during that important moment, he couldn't get it up for her? Their self-esteem would be shredded to bits, and he didn't want that to happen. His job was about helping people in their heat, not ruining it.

He did need a break to figure this little problem out first.

Right at that moment, a phone buzzed. Roy first looked at his work phone but there was no message to be seen, so, he grabbed his other phone and an unfamiliar number appeared on the screen. He was hopeful when he saw it as his private phone never got to receive a lot of messages, and especially not from phone numbers he didn't know.

Could it be?

Roy, I finally know who you are. It took me three days, but I figured it out. Can we please talk?

"Yes!" He laughed. It was her! Should he answer right away? Or did that seem needy? "Oh what the hell," he told himself.

Krissy, good job. I knew you could do it. I really would love to meet with you and catch up. When? I'm on a break from work, so I have plenty of time.

After Roy hit send, he called Xelesia to cancel all further appointments. He felt sorry for the other clients, but he knew some other good escorts, so his clients could use their services in the meantime. Xelesia didn't understand one bit of it, but she didn't ask or say anything. The woman was probably happy to be on break too.

Impatiently, he looked at his phone every fucking two seconds. He had looked up Krissy on social media at least a hundred times the last two days, just to look at her picture. Sadly, her account was set on private so Roy had to be content with this tiny photo. Pathetic as he was, after the hundredth time, he took a screenshot, so he could also enlarge it. He felt like a stalker sometimes. When looking at it right now, a message came in.

Tonight?

Tonight? Krissy had sent! Tonight! Eagerly, Roy started texting back.

Yes, tonight would be great. I can't wait to see you. I've been thinking about you for the past few days and I...

"No, that's too needy." He erased his unsent message.

Yes, shall I be with you at 8? We could eat out or stay indoors. Whatever you want.

Roy looked puzzled at his own message. What if Krissy thought he meant "stay in" as in "stay in and fuck"? Of course, he wouldn't mind doing that, but he didn't want Krissy to think he only was good for that.

"No." He said and deleted his message again.

Yes, you want to have some dinner? I could pick you up at 8?

That was perfect, and he sent it to her. The reply came after half a minute.

Actually, I don't really like to eat out. How about you come here and I will cook for you. Be here at 7.

Roy bit his lip and smiled like an idiot. His heart was beating so fast.

Great, see you tonight at 7.

9

<u>Krissy's burned</u>

<u>Chicken</u>

Roy waited in his car. It was 06:42 pm now, so he was too early. It took all his will-power not to run upstairs to Krissy's apartment right now, but he didn't want to arrive fifteen minutes before the spoken time.

God... He still couldn't believe he was going to eat dinner at her place. And it was a dinner the woman made herself! That somehow felt extra special.

The alpha played some on his phone, killing the time. He sighed after a few minutes. Should he just go already? A little bit earlier wasn't that wrong, right?

He looked into the car's mirror once more, checking himself out, before he opened the door and stepped out.

===

"Oh, fuck!" Krissy yelled when she burned her hand on the frying pan. She grunted out of frustration. Why the hell did she invite Roy for dinner when she can't cook shit?!

Ok, that wasn't entirely true, she could cook a little. But why was she going through so much trouble to make some fancy meal that was clearly way above her head?! The whole kitchen was 1 big mess!

She looked at the time. It was 6.50 pm.

"It's ok, Krissy, you still got a couple of minutes," she told herself, but right after she had pronounced the last word, the doorbell rang. "Oh shit, what should I do?"

She couldn't just pretend she wasn't there. She also couldn't clean up this mess that fast...so, she had no other choice then to face the consequences of her own stupidity. With her head shaking, she walked to the door and opened it.

"Hey," she said to the alpha in front of her. Damn, the man looked so fine again!

Roy's eyes grew wide and his lips curled upwards as Krissy looked at him with a face full of stains and pieces of food in her hair.

"Is everything going ok here?" Roy asked and it seemed like the man was holding in his laughter.

Krissy took a step to the side to show Roy the kitchen. "I don't know, you tell me..." The omega said embarrassed.

The whole kitchen was one exploded mess. There were dripping spoons, and pots that were boiling over. The picture didn't look complete without some smoke, so that was there too, and lets not forget the burned stench.

"Jesus," Roy laughed.

Krissy ran back to the kitchen and turned off the stove. "I'm sorry. Things went a little different then I had planned them. I wanted to cook you a nice dinner to say thanks for all those years ago, yet, this is what you get." Krissy pricked a fork in the black object that was lying in the frying pan and showed it to her guest.

"What is it?"

"Chicken."

"That's chicken?!"

"Well, it was chicken. It's supposed to be chicken... Now, it's fucking black! Look at it, Roy," she said while waving the lump of blackened food in the air. "Why are you standing there, come inside."

"I think you should apologize to the poor creature," Roy said and he stepped inside.

"I'm sorry. I'm so sorry, chicken, I messed you up! I violated your body and I'm sorry!" Krissy may have said it laughingly, but she did mean it. She hated it when food was spoiled.

"I've never seen such a messed up kitchen in my life," Roy said with twinkling eyes. He closed the door and chuckled before he burst out in laughter.

"Shall we just order food in?" Krissy suggested.

"I think that's a good idea. And maybe you want to clean yourself up a bit too."

===================================

15 minutes later, dinner was ordered and Krissy came back out of the bathroom. She then sat down next to Roy on the couch, and the only thing he could think of was: Oh my God. How could she be so perfect? Her scent was heavenly and she was *so* gorgeous and cute and sexy. Even when she had opened the door, looking like a mess, he found her adorable.

His breath hitched while she looked at him with those big beautiful eyes and suddenly he started to hiccup. "*Hic*! Oh.." He shamefully laughed. "Sorry, *hic*! I need to drink some water. *Hic*!" he said, taking a few big gulps of water.

"You need to think about what you ate yesterday. What did you have for dinner?" Krissy asked.

"Errrr... rice and beef. *Hic*!" Roy said.

"And the day before?"

"Pizza."

"And now we again ordered pizza! You should have said so." Krissy had been the one who wanted the pizza, but Roy didn't care. He would eat pizza every day if she wanted it.

"It's ok. *Hic*!" I like pizza."

"And what did you eat the day before?"

Roy thought long until he remembered. "Noodles." *And you, Krissy, I ate you too...* He thought it, but he didn't say it.

"And the day before?"

He tried to remember, but he really didn't know anymore.

"I can't remember, Krissy."

The omega smiled. "Maybe not, but your hiccup is gone."

"I guess it is. Thanks to you."
See? She was amazing!

"Ok, let's talk first." Krissy said. "The pizzas will be delivered in about 30 minutes so we have some time left. So, Roy, it seems like we have a history together."

"We do, yes." When Krissy's arm touched his, he almost fainted.

"You know, I kept your jacket for a long period, but I'm afraid I did throw it away after a while. I'm sorry. I brought it with me to school, but I never saw you again. I heard you were moved?"

Roy laughed. "That thing would be too big for me now, anyway."

"Probably yes.. You look...different." Krissy stated. "So, did you move? Why didn't you ever return to school?"

Roy turned a little more towards her.

"Back then, my parents were debating on moving to Europe for my father's job, for a little while longer already. But then...something happened to our family that made the decision easier for them, so we left, just like that... I heard it the moment I came home after I brought you home.

"That must have been a shitty time, leaving your home and whole life like that," Krissy said.

"It was a bummer, yes. To leave my friends here, going to some place where they have a different culture. Thank God, we went to the United Kingdom, so I could speak the language." Not to mention how absolutely awful it was for him to leave his crush behind. Roy knew Krissy probably had a difficult period back then as well. "And you? Your life changed that day as well..."

"Me finding out I was an omega..? Yeah, it was quite a shock."

"You are ok with it now?" Roy asked.

Krissy nodded. "Yeah, I am."

"You know, I'm actually the only alpha in my family. Both my parents and sister are all omega's." Roy told.
Krissy's mouth fell open for a second. "Really? Your father is an omega?"

It wasn't impossible for male omegas to have children but it didn't happen all too often. Especially not males that carried their babies.

"Yeah. My mother gave birth to my sister, who's 3 years older than I am. There was some sorta complication when she was born and another childbirth was too difficult for my mom, so when my parents wanted another baby, one of my mother's eggs was fertilized with my father's semen and placed into my father. And here I am."

"That's...amazing," Krissy replied.

"Well that's one of the beauties about being an omega male, I guess." Roy said. "There aren't many other good things to it."

"I know. Being a female omega sometimes sucks, I can't even imagine being a male...So, you're well familiar with omegas then."

"God, yes. And they always were in heat together, starting at the same time. It was horrible up to a point that I had to escape the house," Roy jokingly told. He could laugh about it now, back then...not so much. He took a gulp of beer and Krissy did the same.

"That...must have been *way* awkward."

"It was. Krissy, if I wouldn't have fled the house, I would be hearing my parents moan 24 hours long. No thanks."

They both laughed.

"Did you keep in touch with your friends?"

"I did, yeah." Roy pursed his lips. "I...I was in love with someone too. I had to leave her behind as well," he explained.

"Oh, that must've sucked."

"It really fucking sucked. I cried so hard."

Krissy softly smiled at him. "Well now you're back in the country. Have you ever visited her again?"

"I saw her the other day...we talked a little."

"Oh, and?"

"I'm in love all over again."

"I see..."

The alpha wondered if he was hallucinating or not. Did Krissy look a little jealous there?

"So, Krissy, what would you say if a guy came up to you, tells you he's been in love with you since forever and then you find out he's working as an escort? I just don't know what to do... I mean I could give up my job easily, as I don't need it, at least not anymore. But I only want to give it up for something *real*, you know?"

Roy was internally dying to know Krissy's answer.

"Well, I w--"

Unfortunately, Krissy was cut off by the sound of the doorbell, the pizza guy stood in front of the door. *Damn it!*

10

<u>*Talking*</u> *and* <u>*Pizza*</u>

~~~KRISSY~~~

While walking back with the hot pizza boxes in my hand, I thought about what Roy had said. He told me he was in love with someone.

It made me feel strange inside.

Was I jealous?

I hoped that wasn't the case, cause it would be totally absurd. I slept with the guy one night, and that was only because I had booked him to have sex with me!

To be honest, I thought a lot about him these last few days. What was the reason he stayed here all night ánd refused my money? He wouldn't do that with everyone, right? Or would he? But why would he do that?

I just didn't get it.

So for the last three days, some strange voice inside my head said that he might like me. And then, I laughed at myself for thinking about it in the first place.

What did I even want to do with these new weird feelings of mine, anyway? What did I expect? The man was working as a prostitute for God's sake! He was having sex with countless people, over and over again. For money.

What he made me feel that night was an illusion, nothing more or less. He probably made everyone feel that special, it was simply his job to do so.

It was pathetic that our time together was the best experience I'd ever had when it came to feel special and loved. In those almost twenty-four hours, he gave me not only hot sex but also affection and tenderness, something I'd never had since I'd never been in a relationship before.

Till three days ago, I had never woken up next to another person, never received a homemade meal, as he made me, fried eggs and all. I'd never been held in someone's strong arms as he held me.

Generally, I slept with people and that was it. But now I got sweet aftercare, and it made me feel good and safe. Ugh...I think I made it a little bigger in my head than it actually was, and this all resulted in me losing sleep over this man.

Why was this fine man an escort? Why?!

God… I needed to snap out of this. Especially now I'd heard that he had feelings for someone.

~~~ R O Y~~~

Why did that damn pizza boy ring the bell at the most crucial moment?!

After Krissy returned with the pizza, she didn't answer my question anymore. And the answer to that question was exactly what I wanted and needed to know! What would Krissy say when a guy told her that he liked her and that guy turned out to be an escort? Of course, we all know who the escort would be in this story…

I debated if I should just ask again or maybe say something like 'where were we before the bell rang?' But the moment was ruined, thanks to the fucking pizza company.

I looked at Krissy who was currently shoving a slice of pizza in her throat. God, I loved it when women just ate. Sometimes, women were always dieting and all that, not able to enjoy a nice meal, but she was stuffing that thing right in there and I loved it. She looked so clueless with that string of melted cheese hanging out of the corner of her mouth. It was insanely cute. I could just eat that string of cheese right while it hung there.

And those sexy plump lips, I could eat them up as well…

No! I shouldn't go down this road. I didn't want Krissy to feel awkward while smelling my scent getting hornier by the second, so I quickly took a big bite of pizza and tried to think about gross things like frogs and paying taxes and bugs.

"Can I ask you something personal?" she asked.

I knew what her question would be as soon as I heard the words *ask* and *personal.*

"Yes, of course," I answered her after I'd swallowed the bite of pizza. I mean this conversation had to happen once, right?

"So... Uhmm..." she started and I saw her struggling with the right words so I thought I'd give her a little help.

"You want to know why I do this job, don't you?"

"Well...yeah, I'm sorry. If you don't want to share it with me, then it's ok!" She immediately apologized, her cheeks blushing a deeper shade of red.

Why was she so adorable?

"No, I don't mind. It's not like the question hasn't been asked before."

"I guess people just try to understand the reason behind it," she explained.

"I actually kind of rolled into it. I moved back to this country when I was twenty-one. My parents weren't pleased and didn't understand why I wanted to go back, but I just did. So, I applied for college with the thought that if I didn't like it, I could always return back to the UK. But I stayed here." I took a sip because my mouth was a little dry. "At some point, I was a little irritated by my father because I didn't feel supported enough, so I refused my parents' money. Of course, after a few months, mine was all spent. So money was reason number one for taking this job. Now, let me get a bite first." I laughed and shoved the last chunk of my pizza slice in my mouth.

"Sure. You want another slice?"

"In a minute," I said with my mouth still full. After I swallowed, I continued. "I got this girl in class who knew about my financial struggles and this one night she called me and asked if I could come over and help her. She turned out to be in heat and wanted an alpha guy she trusted to help her, so...I helped her out... Afterwards, she stuffed a tiny roll of cash into my hands, which I refused. I never wanted her money. However, she was very persuasive telling me I should take it for the gas I used to come to visit her and all that and in the end, I took it with the idea that I helped her with what she needed and she helped me with what I needed. This way, I at least could pay my rent."

"Ok," Krissy replied. That was all she said. "And the second reason?" she then asked after a short awkward silence.

"Well, the second reason is also the reason that I'm still doing it. It's because people say I'm good at what I do. They say they really feel helped in the end and I like that. I said our family moved away to Europe because of family issues right?"

Krissy nodded.

"It's because of something that had happened to my sister. I heard it all when I came back from driving you home and before my parents told me we would emigrate. The night before, she was out with a friend, and she suddenly fell into heat. It wasn't her first heat but it was an unexpected one. Without telling too much detail right now cause I really don't feel like it...she was raped that night. Not by one alpha, but by a whole group..."

"Oh my god."

"Heat and rut are dangerous things." It pained me to think about it again. "My sister wasn't in her right mind when she entered that alley on her way home from the club. And even though her mouth screamed no to them, her scent said different things. It took her a long time to process everything. She felt like she was at fault, you know?" Krissy nodded and laid her hand on mine, so gently. "People can call me nasty because of my job, but at least I try to help them. I give them the solace they need when they are in heat, like you were too. Some people call me a hypocrite and say that if I want to help, I should do it for free, but my fee is very low and I just make enough money to pay my bills and pay my assistant's salary, that's pretty much it. I don't exploit omegas. I just need to eat too. The alpha's in the alley, the ones who took my sister, they were the nasty ones."

I felt angry thinking about it all over again.

"I... I don't know what to say," Krissy said. "But I understand you."

"Well...then answer my previous question. What would you do if a guy, that you maybe like, told you he loved you but you know he is working as a prostitute? Will he have a chance when it comes to love? Will someone like me have a chance?"

I guess, feeling angry and irritated, thinking about my sister's unfortunate story, made me brave enough to ask her again

"I actually thought about that a lot for the past three days. I thought t--" All of a sudden, her eyes grew wide and her cheeks turned red again. She looked at me, like she had said something wrong and just got caught for it.

Then it hit me.

Why did she think about such a thing for the last three days? Why would she? Could...she...?

"Krissy...do you...like me?"

"...!"

She didn't answer.

But she didn't deny it either!

Ok, this was it! I didn't think about it any longer and decided to just pour my heart out to her. I couldn't go on like this any longer. I mean, my dick didn't even cooperate anymore. I grabbed her hand in mine and she looked at me with wide eyes.

"That person I told you about, the one I was in love with before I left? That person was you, Krissy. You didn't know who I was in school, but I have been in love with you for longer, Krissy. Even long before I drove you home that day. And, oh God, I was so thankful I got to do that. When I was in Europe, the feeling maybe ebbed away a little but it was always there. I never forgot you and it certainly revived when I saw you again this week. I...I wasn't even able to sleep with someone else after you, hence my break..."

"...?!"

She looked at me with an open mouth. Why didn't she answer me?

I got scared, hoping that me telling her wasn't a mistake!

11

Pros and cons

HE COULDN'T BELIEVE HE SAW HER TODAY. THIS MUST HAVE BEEN THE LUCKIEST SATURDAY OF HIS LIFE! NOW HE COULD SEE HER 6 DAYS THIS WEEK, INSTEAD OF 5!

WITH DREAMY EYES BEHIND THICK BLACK-RIMMED GLASSES, HE LOOKED AT THE OTHER SIDE OF THE RESTAURANT, WHERE SHE WAS CURRENTLY HAVING LUNCH.

SHE LAUGHED OUT LOUD. HER LAUGH, HER SMILE... OF COURSE, THAT SMILE! SHE WAS JUST SÓ PERFECT.

BEFORE SHE ENTERED THE RESTAURANT, ROY SAW HER DOING SOME SHOPPING WITH HER GRANDMOTHER AND KRISSY CARRIED ALL THE BAGS. SHE HAD AT LEAST 6 BIG SHOPPING BAGS IN HER HANDS WHILE THE OLD LADY HAD NONE. SHE WOULDN'T LET HER GRANNY CARRY ANY. SHE WAS SUCH A SWEETHEART.

ROY FELT THE BUTTERFLIES FLAPPING WILDLY INSIDE HIS STOMACH.

KRISSY WASN'T ONLY THE MOST BEAUTIFUL BUT ALSO THE SWEETEST AND THE MOST GENTLE. SHE HAD LITERALLY NO FLAWS IN HIS EYES.

THE CHUBBY ALPHA SIGHED, HIS CHIN RESTING INTO THE PALM OF HIS HAND, WHILE HE SUPPORTED HIS ELBOW ON THE SMALL DINING TABLE AT THE OTHER SIDE OF THE RESTAURANT. HIS LIPS CURLED UPWARDS WHILE LOOKING AT HIS CRUSH, WHO JUST TOOK A BITE OF PASTA.

THROUGH THE WINDOW, THE SUNLIGHT SHINED UPON KRISSY'S HAIR LIKE A HALO. FITTING FOR SUCH AN ANGEL.

"ROY?...ROY?!"

"HM?" ROY SNAPPED OUT OF IT, CAME BACK TO THE REAL WORLD, AND LOOKED AT AN ANGRY BLAKE.

"I AM TALKING TO YOU FOR THE PAST FEW MINUTES AND YOU HAVE NOT ONCE ANSWERED ME BACK. LIKE, HELLOOOOOO?!"

"I'M SORRY, UHM..WHAT DID YOU SAY?" ROY ASKED WHILE HIS EYES KEPT TURNING BACK AT THE OBJECT OF HIS INTEREST. OH GOD, SHE WAS JUST SO WONDERFUL!

"ROY!" BLAKE YELLED ONCE MORE.

"BLAKE, HE IS LURKING AT THAT GIRL FROM THE OTHER CLASS AGAIN," KEVIN SAID.

"I WAS NOT," ROY LIED.

"SURE...YOU WEREN'T AT ALL," KEVIN REPLIED, ROLLING HIS EYES.

"JESUS CHRIST! STOP BEING A PUSSY AND STEP UP TO THAT GIRL. PLEASE, DO IT FOR THE SAKE OF US ALL!" BLAKE SAID.

==

Roy rubbed his face into the palm of his hands. Was it stupid that he had told Krissy his feelings? He just blurted it out. No, that wasn't really true, he also wanted to tell her.

But after he did, things had gotten a little awkward. He could just burst into tears, thinking about it again. After he confessed, Krissy just kept looking at him with wide eyes and wide mouth.

When she didn't react to his love declaration, Roy said that Krissy could best let the words sink in and that they'd leave it at that for the night. They then ate in awkwardness and talked about unimportant things before Roy took off, way earlier than he thought he would.

Now, it was 4 a.m. and he couldn't sleep. He could only think about how things could have been if he'd kept his big mouth shut! On the other hand, it felt good he had finally said it. FINALLYafter all these years! It was the first time he'd ever told someone these feelings. He hadn't even told his friends back then, though they seem to know.

He grabbed his phone and read the messages Krissy had sent the other day once more. Over and over again, he read then, like some pathetic person. He wanted to text her so badly, but he didn't know what to say, so he thought it was best to just let things be for now. He didn't wanna stalk her when she needed time.

After he went to the bathroom and crawled back in bed, he plugged in his phone, laid it on the bedside table, and closed his eyes. He was going to sleep now!

When he almost drifted into sleep, he heard a ping coming from his phone and Roy quickly grabbed it. The ping came with a message, one that brought a smile to his face and would keep him up the rest of the night...

==

Krissy looked at her list. Yes, she made a list and she facepalmed herself for it.

PROS:
- SWEET AND GENTLE

- HONEST

- HOT LIKE HELL

- SEX IS MIND-BLOWING

- SAYS HE LIKES ME

- INDEPENDENT

- HELPFUL

- SAYS HE IS WILLING TO QUIT HIS JOB

HARDWORKING

CONS:

- HARDWORKING

- WRONG JOB

It was 3 o'clock in the middle of the night and she was busy with this instead of sleeping.

If she could turn back time, she would. The way she handled Roy's confession was just too dumb. But she was just confused! She'd lie if she said she didn't like Roy because she did him. She liked him a lot. Probably. At least, she thought she did. Ugh! She just didn't know anything about love or relationships. Or about going out with a prostitute!

Roy did say he was willing to give up the job for the right person and for something real. Was she that person? And what was something real?

She most certainly wouldn't want to be in a relationship with an escort, however, she would be able to live with the fact that prostitution was in his past. But *no way* her partner could fuck other people while being in a relationship with her!

Roy had asked for a chance, and after thinking about it for hours and hours, she concluded that she wanted to give Roy that chance.

The clock said 4 o'clock when Krissy reached for her phone and started typing a long text. Without overthinking, she sent it.

1 minute later, she saw the word "read" coming up, so she knew that Roy was reading it at that very moment. Krissy felt nervous and read her own message again.

ROY, I'M SORRY I DIDN'T RESPOND TO YOUR CONFESSION, EARLIER. I WAS JUST A LITTLE BIT IN SHOCK ABOUT THIS WHOLE SITUATION, ALSO ABOUT MY OWN FEELINGS. I KNOW I'M A COWARD TO TELL YOU THIS IN A MESSAGE BUT BEAR WITH ME PLEASE. THESE PAST FEW DAYS, I DID THINK ABOUT YOU. BUT I'M JUST SO CONFUSED ABOUT WHY I HAVE THESE FEELINGS. IF YOU STILL WANT ME, I WANT TO FIND OUT TOGETHER WHAT THE FUTURE CAN BRING US, USING YOUR WORK BREAK AS A TEST... TO LOOK IF THIS IS REAL. IF IT IS, I CAN'T BE IN A RELATIONSHIP WITH YOU WHILE YOU ARE STILL DOING THIS JOB. YOUR BREAK WILL HAVE TO BE PERMANENT THEN. I KNOW I CAN'T FORCE YOU, BUT I'LL ASK YOU TO DO THAT. IF YOU ARE OK WITH WHAT I ASK, THEN I WOULD LIKE US TO GO ON AN OFFICIAL DATE. XXX KRISSY.

Was it ok? The message looked kind of stupid now she read it again. What would Roy say? Why didn't he answer back? Oh God, what if he was mad?! It was night also, why did she send it in the middle of the night, when normal people slept?! What if she had woken him up?!

Krissy cursed herself and regretted the fact that she had sent the message, but then, an incoming message popped up.

KRISSY, I AM SO HAPPY RIGHT NOW. YOU DON'T HAVE
TO FEEL SORRY. YOU DON'T HAVE TO FEEL LIKE A
COWARD EITHER. I SAY YES TO YOUR REQUEST.
PLEASE TELL ME WHEN YOU ARE FREE, I REALLY
LOOK FORWARD TO THAT DATE.

Krissy smiled and bit her lip, texting him back:

THANKS. I THINK IT'S BEST THAT I DON'T COOK FOR
YOU ANYMORE. SHALL I VISIT YOU THIS TIME? OR DO
YOU WANT TO GO SOMEWHERE?

When she was younger, her heats weren't regular and this
one time, she unexpectedly got into one, while dining at a
restaurant. It was like the horror at school all over again.
Ever since then she didn't want to go out to dinner. Maybe
she should overcome it.

Roy had texted back:

NO, YOU TOLD ME YOU RATHER DIDN'T WANT TO GO
OUT. I WANT YOU TO FEEL AS COMFORTABLE AS
POSSIBLE. PLEASE SAY YOU ARE AVAILABLE
TOMORROW.

That alpha was always so thoughtful. Krissy thought about
Roy's reasons for doing his job and even they were noble.
How was that alpha such a good man?

Eagerly, Krissy's fingers began to type her next text, wearing
a huge grin on her face.

I AM, SO, TOMORROW IT IS. YOUR PLACE OR MY PLACE? I WANT TO SEE YOUR PLACE TOO BUT YOU CAN ALSO COME HERE AGAIN IF YOU WANT.

The next text Krissy got was an address and a happy Roy who said he really was looking forward to seeing each other again.

12

A seven years old card

It was valentine's day.

Roy had tried to put in lenses to look as best as possible for Krissy, but his eyes hurt like hell so he was back to wearing his usual thick black glasses again. He wore the best clothes he owned and had something hidden within the inside pocket of his jacket... A card with a handwritten text that declared his love for her.

And now the moment came that he stood there, looking at the object of his affection while finding the courage to give her said card.

Krissy was smiling brightly and laughing with her friends, making Roy's knees turn into jelly, like always.

The alpha decided that he should wait for a better moment, as he couldn't just walk up to the girl right now while she was surrounded by her friends. But then, just when Roy wanted to turn around, Krissy's friends went on and left Krissy behind.

This was his chance!

The chubby guy blew out a big breath and sucked in another one before he slowly approached his crush. Right, when he was almost there, another guy came and handed a card to Krissy first. Roy was too late... And so, he never dared to give his card that day, not after Krissy already received one from that handsome popular soccer player.

Will the alpha ever get a chance again?

================================

"Why would you want to work for me?" Blake asked over the phone.

Roy had him on speaker while he was picking out his clothes. He decided he would go casual today. Just a t-shirt with loose pants.

"Because I'm gonna look for another job, but I need some time to find that job. So, do you need a new bartender or not?"

"You quit selling your body?" Blake asked, a little surprised.

"Please, Blake, just answer me. I will explain it to you another time, not now. " Roy whined.

"I can't pay you a good salary."

Blake had just opened up his bar and he was still in debt, Roy knew that. "That's ok, you don't have to! Please, man?" Roy asked with the saddest and soft gentle voice he could.

"If you are sure you want it... Next Saturday will be you first workday, six pm."

"Yes! Thanks, bud, you're a good friend!"

"Yeah, yeah..." Blake mumbled before he hung up the phone.

Now that was settled, Roy just needed to wait for about thirty minutes till the clock would finally hit seven o'clock, and Krissy would ring his doorbell.

The alpha had been whistling all day. He was so happy! This afternoon, he went to the hairdresser to get a new haircut. Then he did some grocery shopping for tonight. He had cleaned his apartment, took a shower, and was getting dressed now.

==

"You are going to see the sex worker tonight?!" Gemma asked, her eyes looking perplexed after her friend told her the news. "Why?!"

"Well, I think I like him... A lot." Krissy answered and put her curling iron back in the drawer. "How do I look?"

"You look hot. But back to that guy, are you crazy?!"

Krissy has known Gemma since college. She was one of her best friends but to be honest, sometimes Gemma had too much of an opinion of her own.

"Look, I know it's a bit strange to you, but he really is very nice and lovely and gentle and so fucking handsome and just a decent man."

"Decent? He's a whore!"

"Ugh, shut up, Gemma. You don't even know him."

"Oh, come on. You know I'm telling the truth. The man fucks everyone when they pay the right amount of cash," Gemma said while shaking her head.

"Listen, I know you're worried for me. But he said he would quit if he and I will work things out, and get into a more serious thing..." Krissy explained while she went to the bathroom to get her teeth brushed.

"Oh, he said! He said… Oh, yeah that's…like ok then. Or not, like that fucking matters! First, see and then believe. I mean…why is he even doing this kind of job in the first place?!" Gemma hollered at her friend.

"None of your business, Gemma!" Krissy yelled back before spitting out the toothpaste.

One minute later Krissy came back walking into the living room and asked, "What is the time now?!"

"Six."

"Oh, then I need to hurry up!"

"You gonna fuck him tonight?" Gemma asked, laying like some lazyass person on the couch.

"Jesus, why do you care?" Krissy asked.

"I'm just asking, you're my friend. You've cleaned yourself for him, didn't you?"

"Oh my God. That's none of your business." Krissy rolled her eyes.

Yes. Yes, she had. She had cleaned herself very, very thoroughly but Gemma didn't need to know that.

There was always the possibility of sex. And if Roy would initiate something tonight, Krissy sure as hell wouldn't refuse. After they had shared a night, she realized that all the sex she had before was just fucking *bad* sex.

"So that's a yes?" Gemma asked.

"Please Gemma, just get the fuck out of my apartment."

=====================================

Roy sat on the couch with a seven years old card in his hands, something he had kept with him all these years.

He debated if he wanted to show it to Krissy. Last time the girl almost had a heart attack when Roy told her about his feelings. But he wanted to show Krissy how deep these feelings were, that they were already so much there, back in school.

The doorbell rang and Roy stood up with a fast-beating heart and walked to the door. With a sweaty palm, he opened the door.

God! The woman was so beautiful. Every time again, she made his mouth slam open in complete awe.

Her hair was worn down but looked different because it seemed a little more curly than usual. She took off her coat and wore a tight short red dress underneath and she stood tall in high heels.

Fuck!

"Krissy, hey," the alpha said.

Krissy was grinning like an idiot too and they stood a little awkward and chuckled together.

"This way," Roy said after he took her coat, hung it on a hook, and before they walked through the hallway. The apartment was simple and kind of small, but clean. "Sit down. Do you want a drink?" Roy asked when they stood before a dark red couch.

"Sure."

~

"Do you like it?" Roy asked hopefully.

"...!"

Krissy's face turned redder by the second. She grabbed the glass of water and took a few sips, coughing in the process.

"Krissy?"

"Yes?" the omega answered with an extremely hoarse voice.

"Is it too spicy for you?"

"I'm so sorry. I don't want you to feel bad since you put effort into it."

"But I don't want you to eat it when you can't handle it. So, this is too spicy for you?!"

Roy was surprised. It actually wasn't that spicy at all...at least, not to him. He didn't want Krissy to feel bad. The poor woman was even starting to sweat.

"I just can't eat anything spicy. Really, I'm a baby like that. I'm so sorry," Krissy explained before she tried to suppress another cough and failed. She quickly took another sip of water.

"It's ok, I'll make you something else," Roy said while he stood up, grabbing Krissy's plate.

God, why did he have to cook this spicy food?! He cursed himself internally.

"You don't have to, Roy," Krissy said.

"But I want to."

~

An hour later they sat on the couch, drinking something stronger than water. During dinner, they had talked about all sorts of things, from movies to family history and from new sports cars to favorite animals.

While Krissy put her glass back on the coffee table, her knee accidentally brushed against Roy's. Like an electric shock, the Alpha felt her warm touch against his leg, giving him

shivers that ran down his spine. Roy swallowed. Now! He
was just gonna do it now!

He sat up straight and opened up the coffee table's drawer.
He picked out a card and placed it in Krissy's hands.

"What's this?" Krissy asked, surprised.

"Please read it...It's more than seven years old," Roy
answered and he blushed lightly, feeling nervous for her
reaction.

"It's for me?"

"Hmm-hmm."

Krissy opened up the envelope. It was slightly wrinkled and
stained. Out came a card with red hearts. The omega folded
it open and started reading.

——

Happy valentine's day, sweet Krissy,

Whenever I see you, I smile.

*I lastly think about you before I fall asleep and firstly when
I wake up.*

You make school fun, just because you are there.

I know I don't have much to offer. I may not look like a prince charming but I'm kind and I would do anything for you. Will you please go out with me?

Xx Roy.

———

"Why did you never give me this back then?" was all that Krissy asked.

"I wanted to, but somebody beat me to it..." Roy sighed and ran his hand through his hair. "I don't know... When I saw you laughing with the person who gave you the card before me, I chickened out."

The alpha's eyes grew large when Krissy grabbed his face between her hands. "I think it was very sweet," she said and she slowly came closer and pressed her lips against the alpha's.

Even though they already went much further than this, it was different now. Now it was *real*.

After a passionate kiss that took both their breaths away, it was Krissy that said: "Will you show me the rest of the house?"

13

Desires

The door slammed open and two people who were aroused beyond words, stumbled inside, their faces glued together while desires were awoken by each other's exciting scents.

Roy had never in his wildest dreams expected this to happen, but it did.

He shoved Krissy against the wall and pulled her dress over her head while she was busy undressing him at the same time. She almost ripped his shirt apart when the piece of clothing didn't cooperate fast enough.

"Ahh...Jesus..." She moaned when Roy's hands slid up from her knees to her inner thighs and beyond.

The alpha plucked her lace panties down, which was already damped from wanting him before he kneeled and licked her inner thighs as he took off his pants and boxers as well.

"Ahh..." Krissy breathed hard when the wet tongue came so close to where she wanted it to be.

But he didn't... Instead, Roy stood up and took her ass in a tight grip, squeezing the soft round cheeks and pulling her hips against his own. His hard clothed erection pressed against her heat. "Are you sure about this?" he asked.

"So sure..." Krissy admitted with a hoarse voice and giggled when he hoisted her up in the air and walked them over to the bed, where he laid her down before walking to the bedside table. Within a few seconds, he rolled a rubber glove over his rock-hard cock.

No more interruptions from now on!

"Oh...Roy..." Krissy moaned when the alpha kissed every inch of her overheated skin.

It was just like a few days ago when he also made her feel so worthy and desirable. They kissed and rolled around in the bed before Roy slid lower, his tongue swirling over her hardening nipples on his path down. When he arrived where he wanted to be, he kissed her hips and thighs and gently laid her legs over his shoulders, widening them and pulling Krissy closer till his mouth was buried between them...

"You taste so good," Roy mumbled before he let his tongue run over her folds and pushed it inside.

"Ahh!"

Krissy's heart raced and pounded on more than one spot inside her body as his mouth sucked on her swelling lips and licked up and down, sometimes pushing inside and out again. She felt high and delirious from the swirling motions that assaulted her clit after some minutes. Krissy never had been this horny in life.

"Roy...I don--"

I don't know how much more I can take, that was what she wanted to say, but she couldn't pronounce the words anymore, as her brain was no longer fitted to make any coherent sentences.

"I... ahh..! R-roy!" she cried out.

While the tongue stirred inside her, the excitement stirred inside the pool of desire that was forming inside her stomach.

She had reached her limit and came loud while her hands ruffled through the alpha's hair. He blinked up at her, his eyes dark and heavy-lidded and that made it even hotter.

Roy made her fall apart, into a thousand pieces under his skilled touch and it was like her orgasm lasted at least half a minute. After that, she slowly regained some consciousness again.

Roy moved back up and laid down next to Krissy, pulling the woman in his embrace and she rested her head on his chest. "Your heartbeat is fast," Krissy said. "That's all on you," Roy said as he caressed Krissy's back with the palm of his hand, making slow long strokes against the spine.

Krissy nuzzled at his chest and she couldn't believe he seemed to smell better every time they met. Suddenly, a pang of jealousy hit her heart, thinking about the fact that Roy must have done this for a lot of people.

"You're thinking about something. What are you thinking?" Roy asked.

"Just...nothing."

"Tell me. I want you to be honest with me. And I'll be honest with you too, always."

Krissy bit her lip. "Well... I just thought about the fact that you had these kinds of moments with a lot of people...while for me...it's really special."

Roy pulled Krissy's face up with his thumb under her chin. "Yes, I've had a lot of sex in my life, I can't lie about that...but it was work. There were never any feelings involved. So, if you think that this is not special for me, you are wrong, because now I do feel. I have feelings for you and I swear to God that this is just as special for me as it is for you. Maybe even more."

Krissy felt a little shy when Roy's eyes gazed at her so intensely. She laid her head flat down again. Roy's skin felt soft and warm against her cheek. She let her hand move towards Roy's hard-on and she grabbed it in a tight grip and pointed it up before she straddled Roy and slowly folded herself over the yearning thick erection.

"Ahhh..." Roy moaned when he felt the heat enveloping him and he looked into Krissy's eyes. This felt so good.

Krissy began to bounce up and down, slowly. Clenching herself around the hard-on. She looked gorgeous. Her big breasts bounced up and down and he caressed them while enjoying her taking the lead. It sure was a sight for sore eyes.

Roy sat up straight so he could hug and kiss her and Krissy pressed her nose against his scent gland and moaned before she steadied herself and vigorously began to move up and down. Roy's cock filled her so well while the alpha licked and sucked on her nipples.

"Ahh... Krissy..." Roy panted.

They pressed their lips together, tongues stroking sensually.

"...I..I'm so close again..." Krissy heavily breathed.

"Come then..." Roy ordered.

Krissy came when she felt Roy's knot forming as the muscles in his penis expanded and pressed against a certain sensitive spot inside her.

They came together.

==

Roy smelled Krissy's neck. Her scent was so calming. This scent was everything he needed in his life.

They hadn't talked much since Krissy arrived. It was from her entering his apartment to reading the letter, to become so desperate for each other they ended up in Roy's bed.

"I closed my company and arranged that I'll work at a friend's bar from this Saturday till I find something else," Roy said while he looked up into Krissy's eyes.

"Really?"

"Of course."

Krissy smiled. "But, how does it make you feel?"

"Well my clients are under the care of a few other great alphas now, so I don't have to worry for them, so things are settled. I want to make this work, Krissy" he said.

"I do too," Krissy replied.

Roy smiled like an idiot. "Let's shower together. We are so dirty right now."

14

Pink

Krissy looked at the thick glossy business card in her hand.

R. Cesar. Alpha escort.

The omega bit her lip when she thought back about that first night. It felt like it was a decade ago, but it had only been one year in the past.

So much had happened in that one year...

A few months after that first night, Krissy had received Roy's mark. In return, she gave Roy a mark as well and they were forever bonded together. as alpha and omega. Mates from that day on. They belonged together, forever and ever.

After that, when they had saved some money and Roy and her could get 2 months off from work, they traveled to Europe together, to visit Roy's family and have their first vacation together. Roy's parents and sister had been so nice, Krissy immediately felt a deep connection with them. The fact that they were omega just like she was, helped.

Roy and she stayed for 2 weeks before they explored Europe for a 1.5 months and returned home again. It was a journey to never forget. They had visited France and climbed the Eiffel Tower, ate waffles in Belgium, and went to see the colorful tulips in the Netherlands. They visited Berlin and Rome and Spain, where Krissy was so impressed with the Sagrada Familia in Barcelona.

Later, Roy was also introduced to Krissy's family. They decided to hide the way they met again. Krissy felt her parents didn't need to know that. They gave their blessings to them, and even Gemma did. Though she still said she didn't like Roy, Krissy knew the girl was lying. She could tell that Gemma thought that Roy was a cool guy. Besides, how could one not think highly of the man? Roy was the best. He even helped Krissy to overcome her not-going-out-to-dinner-fear.

"Why would you rather not go out on a date?" Roy asked.

"Well... What happened to me in school, me drenching my pants with slick, that also happened while eating at a restaurant, a few years ago. So now I'm just a little traumatized I guess."

"I'm sorry, it must have been hard. Your heat, doesn't that come like every 4 weeks?"

Roy sat down opposite Krissy. They were eating breakfast, even though it was already 2 p.m.

"Well it does now, but in the past, it didn't. I was having irregular heats for a few years and slowly they came more regularly. Mostly I could feel it coming but I never was 100% when it might hit me. But I was also just dumb that day. I felt a little off all day long but I really wanted to go cause I hadn't seen Gemma for a while and we would eat together." Krissy explained.

Roy lovingly smiled when he leaned towards Krissy and rubbed off a few crumbs that stuck at the corner of Krissy's mouth.

"Oh, am I eating like a pig again?"

"No. You're cute." Roy said, showing his killer smile. He sat down on his chair again. "But what if it was with me? Would you be willing to try? Let's go together. When you're having a hard time, we will immediately leave. I just don't think you should avoid this forever. You're young, you should be able to go out and have fun."

Krissy knew Roy had a point. "Ok, when you are there for me, I guess I can give it a try."

Roy really had it all, the whole package, he was just great!

He worked at Blake's for almost a whole year because he couldn't find something else, but he couldn't do it anymore. He needed to do something else. It just wasn't his type of work and Krissy saw him getting unhappier by the day.

Krissy laid the business card down on her coffee table. Her eyes got blurry vision as they were teared up. She felt so emotional. Why did she even keep that piece of paper? It was time to throw it away. She didn't want to be reminded of Roy's escort days anymore.

~

"Which flavor?"

"Doesn't matter, surprise me," Krissy said to the man holding the ice cream scoop. She looked at all that luscious cream in all those colors and every single one of the flavors looked delicious to her.

While waiting for her surprise ice cream, she sat down at the bar inside the empty ice cream saloon. It was a beautiful place with lots of tables and where one could also order cakes and pies and doughnuts and other sweets, but it was completely empty, nobody sat there but her.

"Here you go."

"Thanks," she said and started licking, her tongue twirling around the soft, sweet, cold cream.

She felt so many things. Maybe because her heat would come in 2 days. She could get very emotional during these times of the month.

"Are you ok?" the man asked while he laid down his ice cream scoop.

"Oh yeah… I'm just emotional."

After a moment, Krissy felt 2 strong hands embracing her from the back and a flyer was laid on the bar, in front of her nose.

"Are you nervous, baby?" the man asked while holding his Krissy tight.

"I'm sorry… I'm just…" she sniffed. "So proud of you, Roy," she said with glossy eyes. "This ice cream is really tasty, just so you know."

Roy laughed. "I know, you already told me many times, love."

Krissy looked around. They had everything ready for the grand opening. All their family and friends would come and they hoped that many customers would also come to check out the new place. Tomorrow was the day of the opening.

A few weeks back, Roy came with his new plan of quitting his job at Blake's and opening his own place and Krissy had been the best supportive girlfriend there was. She was so proud. "I Love you."

"Not as much as I love you," Roy said and he nibbled on her ear.

Krissy looked at the flyer. Not a black business card anymore, but a pink flyer this time with lots of colors.

In purple curly letters there stood:

Roy's ice cream parlor.
Scoops, shakes, doughnuts, and cakes.

THANK YOU

PLESASE LIKE AND REVIEW